THE JUSTICE LEAGUE™ SAVES CHRISTMAS!

By Steve Foxe

Illustrated by Pernille Ørum

Random House 🏠 New York

Copyright © 2021 DC Comics.
JUSTICE LEAGUE and all related characters and elements
© & ™ DC Comics. WB SHIELD: ™ & © Warner Bros. Entertainment Inc. (s21)

All rights reserved. Published in the United States by Random House Children's Books, a division of Penguin Random House LLC, 1745 Broadway, New York, NY 10019, and in Canada by Penguin Random House Canada Limited, Toronto. Random House and the colophon are registered trademarks of Penguin Random House LLC.

rhcbooks.com

ISBN 978-0-593-38082-6 (trade)

MANUFACTURED IN CHINA

10 9 8 7 6 5 4 3 2 1

Format development and production by Red Bird Publishing Ltd., UK

One quiet December evening, Cyborg and The Flash were stationed at the Hall of Justice, keeping an eye out for anything that might disturb the peaceful holiday season, when they got a distress call! The Super Heroes couldn't believe their eyes. It was Santa Claus!

"All my reindeer have colds," Santa explained. "Without them, I'll **never** be able to deliver these presents. The only team of Super Heroes who can help me save Christmas is the Justice League!"

"You've got it!" Cyborg said, and he sent out the emergency signal. "With Christmas on the line, there's no time to waste!"

Within moments, from all around the world, Superman, Batman, Wonder Woman, Aquaman, The Flash, Cyborg, and Green Lantern were on their way to the North Pole!

The Justice League soon reached its destination.
"We're here to help," Wonder Woman said.

"I sure could use it," Santa said. He was
relieved that the Super Heroes had arrived so
quickly. "I'm already behind schedule. And look
at all these presents that need to be delivered!"

"I think my Invisible Jet can help with that," Wonder Woman said.

Santa scratched his head, considering the unusual vehicle. "I'm not sure I can steer something I can't see," he admitted.

"I'll do the flying," Wonder Woman said with a chuckle. "You just focus on the presents."

As the Invisible Jet zoomed quietly over town after town, Santa and his newest "elves" delivered presents to the children below. "Not too fast, Wonder Woman!" Cyborg shouted. "I don't want to miss any chimneys!"

While the Invisible Jet flew across the sky, The Flash raced through busy city streets in another part of the world. He delivered countless presents in the blink of an eye.

"This should help make up for lost time," the Scarlet Speedster said with a grin.

Aquaman plowed through the waves on a sleigh built for the sea.

"I'm having a whale of a good time!" he shouted, enjoying every second of playing Santa. "The entire ocean is on the nice list this year!"

Meanwhile, in yet another part of the world, the weather took a turn for the worse. When the Invisible Jet had trouble making it through the storm, Green Lantern helped guide the sleigh. Like with a certain famous reindeer, her glowing green light lit their path.

"It doesn't matter how dark and snowy it is," Green Lantern proclaimed, "no gifts shall go undelivered tonight!"

Meanwhile, Batman visited house after house, making sure that on this special night, he would strike **cheer** into the hearts of the boys and girls of Gotham City as he left presents and filled stockings with treats.

Superman didn't bother pulling a sleigh.
Instead, he carried Santa's giant bag of
presents over one super-strong shoulder.
Just like Santa, Superman knew who
was sleeping and who was awake.
Shhhh. . . .

In just one night, the Justice League traveled across the entire planet delivering gifts. Wonder Woman left gifts for the Amazons on Paradise Island. Aquaman took presents to the underwater city of Atlantis. The Flash's furry friends in Gorilla City would also find something in the morning. And Superman personally delivered a gift to one of the Justice League's closest friends—Billy Batson.

They even snuck into the Legion of Doom's headquarters. After all, heroes can't leave **anyone** out during the holidays . . .
. . . not even villains.

At dawn on Christmas morning, Santa and the Justice
League returned to the North Pole.
"I can't believe you do this by yourself every year,"
Green Lantern told Santa. "We delivered every present . . .
but it wasn't easy!"

"Well, you delivered **almost** every present," Santa replied. "Looks like there are just seven gifts left . . . one for each of you."

"You're the best, Santa!" Cyborg exclaimed along with the rest of the heroes. "You should join the Justice League—I bet we could use **your** help, too!"

"Thank you for the kind invitation," Santa replied. "But my reindeer are looking better already, and now I have to start getting ready for **next** Christmas!"